Classic Tales of Terror

Stories of suspense by

H.G. Wells

Robert Louis Stevenson

Saki

Edgar Allan Poe

W. W. Jacobs

A.M. Burrage

SCHOLASTIC INC.

New York Toronto London Auckland Sydney
Mexico City New Delhi Hong Kong

Robert Louis Stevenson's "Dr. Jekyll and Mr. Hyde" adapted by Scholastic Inc.
was published in SCHOLASTIC SCOPE LITERATURE: LEVEL 3, © 1979 by Scholastic Inc.
Alfred McLelland Burrage's "The Waxwork" from SOMEONE IN THE ROOM
adapted by J.S.F. Burrage was published in
SCHOLASTIC SCOPE LITERATURE: LEVEL 3, © 1979 by Scholastic Inc.

Printed in the U.S.A.

ISBN 0-439-05684-5

4 5 6 7 8 9 10 23 06 05 04 03 02 01

Table of Contents

Arthur Wedderburn was bored—until an exotic flower brought terror into his life. . . .

The Strange Orchid

Based on the story by H.G. Wells

Arthur Wedderburn was a lonely man, and his life was very boring. He had inherited just enough money to support himself. He didn't have a job, or a wife, or children. He might have spent his time collecting stamps or writing poetry, but, instead, he grew orchids.

He had his own greenhouse, and he liked to go to orchid sales. Buying orchids gave him a secret thrill. He could buy a brown, dried-up root, not knowing exactly what kind of orchid it would be. Then, if he was lucky, it might grow into a spectacular new kind of flower.

One morning, Wedderburn was eating breakfast with his housekeeper, Lucille. As he wiped his mouth, he said, "I have a feeling that something is going to happen to me today."

"Oh, don't say that!" she said. Lucille always thought that "something happening" meant trouble.

"I don't mean that anything bad will happen. It's just that there's an orchid sale in London today, and they're selling some plants that a man named Batten found in the East Indies."

“Is that the same Batten you told me about the other day,” Lucille asked, “the one who died?”

“Yes,” said Wedderburn. “I wonder why nothing exciting ever happens to *me*. Things happen to other people. Look at Batten, for instance. He was only 36 when he died. By then, he’d been married twice. He almost died of malaria four times. Once he killed an elephant. Once he was shot with a poisoned dart. In the end, jungle leeches killed him.”

“I’d rather not have so much excitement,” said Lucille. “Which reminds me of something: If you’re going to London, you’d better take an umbrella. It looks like rain.”

When Wedderburn got back from the orchid sale, he was excited. He had bought several orchid roots, which he showed Lucille. As he touched one of the roots, he said, “No one knows what kind of orchid this is, but it was the last one that Batten ever collected.”

“I don’t like the look of it,” said Lucille, making a face. “It looks like a spider playing dead.”

Wedderburn smiled at her. “It’s hard to judge orchids by their roots. It may turn out to be a very beautiful flower. I’m going to plant it tomorrow.”

Then Wedderburn frowned a little. “They found Batten lying dead in a swamp, with one of these orchids crushed under his body. He’d had some kind of fever, and I guess he must have fainted. By the time they found him, jungle leeches had drained every drop of

blood from his body. Finding this plant may have cost him his life!"

"How awful to die in some swamp," Lucille said.

"He died doing what he wanted to do," Wedderburn said, "and it does make this plant especially interesting, don't you think?"

The next few days were busy for Wedderburn. He spent hours watching the orchid for any signs of life. When it began to grow, he was so excited that he took Lucille out to the greenhouse to show it to her.

"This is a bud," he pointed out. "Soon there will be leaves over here, and those little things are roots that grow above the soil. Like the roots below, they take in both air and moisture."

"They look like little white fingers reaching out," she said, "and I don't like them."

"I have never seen an orchid quite like this," Wedderburn said. "Perhaps it will make me famous."

After one more visit, Lucille refused to go into the greenhouse anymore. By then, the outside roots of the orchid had grown about a foot long. They reminded her of the long arms that reached out after her in her worst nightmares. She left Wedderburn to admire the plant by himself.

The orchid was beginning to grow leaves now—broad, shiny, and dark green. Near the stems Wedderburn noticed little dots of dark red. He had never seen leaves like that before.

Every day, he went to see if a flower had bloomed. At last, the great day arrived. When he went inside the greenhouse, there was a rich, sweet smell perfuming the air.

Wedderburn hurried over to the strange orchid, which now held three great white blossoms. The orchids had streaks of gold along the edges, and the centers were purple mixed with gold. He knew at once that this was a completely new kind of orchid.

Wedderburn was so happy, but he also felt strange, almost dizzy. The smell was so sweet, and the greenhouse was so hot! He wanted to check to see if the temperature was right. He took a step—and suddenly the brick floor seemed to move up and down. Then the whole greenhouse seemed to swing up sideways, as he fainted.

At four-thirty, Lucille had tea ready, but Wedderburn did not come in as usual. "He must be studying that horrible orchid," she told herself.

She went to the greenhouse, opened the door, and called his name. She heard no reply. She did notice that the air was very stuffy and smelled very sweet. Then she saw Wedderburn lying on the brick floor.

He was lying, face upward, at the foot of the strange orchid. The outside roots no longer swayed in the air like arms waiting to clutch something. Instead, they clung to Wedderburn's chin, neck, and hands. A drop of blood trickled down his cheek.

Lucille ran to him and tried to pull him away from the leech-like roots. She snapped off two of them, and their sap dripped red. The smell of the blossoms began to make her dizzy. She knew she must not faint, so she ran outside and breathed in cool, fresh air. Then she took a flowerpot and smashed the windows at the end of the greenhouse.

She hurried back to Wedderburn and tugged at his body. The strange orchid crashed to the floor, but it still hung on to him. She had no choice but to drag them both outside the greenhouse.

Then she grabbed some garden shears and cut through the sucker roots one by one. Finally, Wedderburn was free, but he was very pale and was bleeding from about a dozen spots.

Just then, a deliveryman came into the garden and headed toward the house. He stopped when he saw Lucille wiping blood from Wedderburn's face. "Go get Dr. Haddon!" she shouted.

"I'm on my way!" he shouted back.

Wedderburn opened his eyes and asked, "What's the matter?"

"You fainted," she explained.

"What about my orchid?" he asked weakly.

"I'll take care of it," she said.

Wedderburn had lost a great deal of blood, but other than that, he was all right. "Just stay in bed for a few days," Doctor Haddon told him.

Then the doctor asked Lucille to show him exactly what had happened. Lucille led him to the greenhouse, where cold air now blew in through the broken windows. The sweet smell was almost gone, and some of the torn roots lay withered on the floor. When the doctor bent to look more closely, one of the roots stirred a little, and he stepped quickly away.

The next day, all of Wedderburn's orchids were dead. The cold wind blowing through the broken windows had killed them. Upstairs, Wedderburn himself was bright and lively, talking about his adventure. At last, something had happened to him.

H.G. WELLS

Herbert George Wells (1866-1946) was one of the world's best science-fiction writers. He studied biology until 1893. Then he started writing novels that put what he knew to work. Two of his best known are *The Time Machine* and *The Invisible Man*.

Wells became even more famous in 1938 when the actor Orson Welles (no relation) turned another of his science-fiction stories, *The War of the Worlds*, into a radio play. The story is about a Martian invasion of Earth. People all over the United States heard the show, thought it was a real newscast, and panicked.

Dr. Jekyll was a good, kind man. Mr. Hyde was evil to the core. But they shared a terrible secret. . . .

Dr. Jekyll and Mr. Hyde

BASED ON THE NOVEL BY ROBERT LOUIS STEVENSON

The man almost didn't seem human. It wasn't just because he was very ugly. It was much worse than that. To me, he had the face of pure evil. I could not look at him without feeling disgust and fear. He was very small and spoke in a husky whisper. His manner was an odd mixture of boldness and fear that, I repeat, seemed less than human.

So how did I meet this awful man? Well, I am a lawyer, and my name is Utterson. One day, as I was walking with my friend Mr. Enfield, we passed a strange house. It had no windows, a badly scratched door, and no bell. Enfield started to tell me a story about the ramshackle old place.

It all began one dark night when he was walking home alone. "I saw two people in front of me," he told me. "A small man was walking this way, and a young girl was running along a cross street. They bumped into each other, and the girl fell down.

"You'll never believe what happened next," Enfield said. "The man attacked the girl. He jumped up and down on her like some kind of animal. Then he tried

to run away, but I chased him and finally caught him. He didn't put up much of a fight, but the hideous look on his face made me break out in a cold sweat.

"I took the man back to the place where he'd hurt the girl. By then, a group of people had gathered around her. They stared at him with hatred, and the child's father looked as if he wanted to kill him," said Enfield. "To save his own skin, the man offered to pay the child's father a hundred pounds.

"I went with the man to get the money. He went inside this same house. After a few minutes, he came out with a check signed by a famous doctor! I figured that it must be a fake, but the bank cashed it. Then I suspected that this awful man must be blackmailing the doctor. How else could he have gotten the check?"

"What was the man's name?" I asked Enfield.

"Edward Hyde," he said.

I didn't have to ask him the name of the doctor. I knew it already. A month before, I had made out a will for Dr. Henry Jekyll. The will said that if Dr. Jekyll died or disappeared, all his money and possessions should go to "his good friend, Edward Hyde."

I never did like this will. Why would Dr. Jekyll just disappear? After I heard Mr. Enfield's story, I liked the will even less. I decided to see this Mr. Hyde and find out for myself what kind of "friend" he was.

I waited across the street from that strange house whenever I could, but for several days, I didn't see Mr.

Hyde. Finally, one night, a small man appeared and walked up to the door. I quickly crossed the street and touched him on the shoulder. “I believe you are Mr. Hyde,” I said.

“That is my name,” he said, drawing back into the shadows, “but what do you want?”

“I am a friend of Dr. Jekyll,” I told him. Then I asked if I could see his face. For a moment, he seemed unsure of what to do, but eventually he stepped into the light. I must say that his face was even more awful than I had imagined.

Mr. Hyde must have seen my look of horror because

he laughed and then darted inside the house. I was left standing outside.

I wanted to warn Dr. Jekyll about his evil "friend." As I walked around the block to Dr. Jekyll's fine house, I realized that the strange house was attached to his! It was, I learned, his workroom, where he tested different kinds of drugs.

When I got to Jekyll's front door, his butler, Poole, answered. "I'm sorry," he said, "but Dr. Jekyll is not at home."

"That's odd," I answered. "I just saw Mr. Hyde go in through the back."

"It's not so odd," said Poole. "Dr. Jekyll has given Mr. Hyde a key. He told me to let the man go in whenever he wants."

I was certain now that Mr. Hyde was blackmailing Dr. Jekyll. What if Hyde found out about Jekyll's will? He would probably murder the doctor to get his hands on all that money!

Two weeks later, I had a chance to see Dr. Jekyll at home. I wondered how this fine man could have anything to do with the awful Mr. Hyde. "I am sure Hyde is dangerous," I told him.

"There's nothing to worry about," Dr. Jekyll assured me. "Mr. Hyde is not as bad as he seems. What's more, I could get him out of my life in a second if that's what I wanted." Then he paused for a second. "Did you ever change my will the way that I asked?"

"I haven't done it yet," I told him, "but I will." I still didn't feel very happy about it.

It turned out, about a year later, that I was right about Mr. Hyde. He murdered an old man on the street one night. A housemaid saw the whole thing from her bedroom window.

"The old man seemed lost," she told the police, "and he stopped Mr. Hyde to ask the way. Suddenly, Mr. Hyde seemed to go crazy and beat the old man to the ground. It killed him instantly."

I went at once to see Dr. Jekyll. He looked deathly ill and could hardly speak, but he managed to say that he had, of course, heard about the murder.

"Are you hiding the murderer?" I demanded. "Is Mr. Hyde somewhere in your house?"

"Utterson," Dr. Jekyll cried, "I swear to you that I will never set eyes on Mr. Hyde again. I am done with him forever."

"How can you be sure?" I asked

He showed me a letter from Mr. Hyde, saying that he was running away and would never bother Dr. Jekyll again.

In the next two months, nothing more was heard of Mr. Hyde, and Dr. Jekyll seemed like his old self. He began to see his friends again, and he gave more time and money to help the poor. His whole face seemed brighter and younger.

Then, suddenly, Dr. Jekyll shut himself up in his house and refused to see anyone.

I stopped by and spoke to his butler, Poole. "How is Dr. Jekyll doing?" I asked.

Poole seemed upset. "He spends most of the time in his workroom," he said. "He hardly ever speaks. I know something serious is bothering him. I just don't know what it is."

I decided to visit Jekyll's old friend, Dr. Lanyon. Perhaps he would know what was troubling Jekyll. When I saw Lanyon, I was shocked. Only a few days before, he had looked fit and well. Now he was very thin, and his hair had turned white.

"I have had a great shock," Dr. Lanyon told me, "and I fear that I will die . . . very soon."

"Dr. Jekyll is ill, too," I said. "Have you seen him?"

Dr. Lanyon's voice shook when he answered me. "Don't talk to me about Dr. Jekyll," he cried. "As far as I'm concerned, he's dead already. If you can't talk about something else, then just leave!"

Two weeks later, Dr. Lanyon was dead. Before he died, he had sent me a letter. I took it out of my safe and reread the envelope: "Open on the occasion of the death or disappearance of Dr. Henry Jekyll."

There was that word again—*disappearance*, the same word Dr. Jekyll had used when he asked me to change his will. I wanted to open the envelope right away, but I knew that I shouldn't. I put it back in my safe and decided to wait.

A few nights later, Dr. Jekyll's butler came to see me. "I can't stand it anymore," he said, shaking with fear. "I believe Dr. Jekyll has been murdered. Please come to his house with me."

I ran out into the street with Poole. It was a wild, windy night, and I had an awful feeling of doom. When we got to Jekyll's house, Poole led me to the workroom, knocked on the door, and called, "Mr. Utterson is asking to see you."

A voice from the workroom said, "Tell him I cannot see anyone."

Poole turned to me. "That wasn't Dr. Jekyll's voice, was it? I don't think so. The last time I was sure that I'd heard his voice was eight days ago. He was crying out to God for help. I'm sure he's been murdered by that man inside—Mr. Hyde!"

"Are you absolutely sure that's Mr. Hyde in there?" I demanded.

"I saw him with my own eyes," Poole said. "He slipped outside once to look for a drug. You know how tall Dr. Jekyll was. *This* man was short and ugly. The moment he saw me, he ran back inside."

I wasn't convinced. "Suppose it was Mr. Hyde, and he did murder Dr. Jekyll. Why wouldn't he run away?"

Poole had an answer for that, too. "The man inside the workroom needs a certain drug. He's sent me all over the city to get more and more of it, but there never seems to be enough."

I had to know the truth. "Jekyll," I called out. "If

you don't open the door, I'll break it down!"

The voice inside cried out, "Utterson, please . . ."

I knew then that Poole was right. It was Mr. Hyde's voice, not Dr. Jekyll's.

"Poole," I said, "down with the door!"

Poole grabbed an axe and smashed the door. We heard a terrible scream from inside. A moment later, we broke in and saw a small, twisted body lying on the floor. I turned it over and looked into the evil face of Edward Hyde. He had killed himself.

Poole and I could not find Dr. Jekyll's body anywhere, but we did find a letter that he had written to me. In it, Dr. Jekyll said that he was sure his end was near. He asked me to read the letter that Dr. Lanyon had sent me. Then if I could bear to know more, I should read a letter from himself which he had locked in his desk. These two letters, he said, would clear up the mystery of Dr. Jekyll and Mr. Hyde.

I went home immediately. First, I read the letter from Dr. Lanyon:

"On January 9, I got a letter from an old friend, Dr. Henry Jekyll. In it he begged me to go to his house and ask for Poole. He wanted the two of us to break into his workroom, remove a drawer from his medicine cabinet, and carry the drawer back to my house.

"At midnight, Jekyll said, a man would come to my house for the drawer, and I should be waiting alone. He begged me not to let him down. He said that his

'honor, sanity, and life' depended on it.

"I was sure that Jekyll had gone out of his mind, but, as a friend, I did what he asked. At midnight, when I heard a knock on my door, I let in a small man with a face that shocked and disgusted me. He could hardly wait for me to give him the drawer, and when I did, he gave a cry of relief.

"Then he gave me a choice. I could let him go without asking any questions, or, if I chose, he would show me something extremely interesting. I said that since I had gone this far, I would see it to the end.

"He then took a jar of red liquid out of the drawer and mixed it with a drug that looked like salt. The liquid began to boil and smoke and finally to change color—from red, to purple, to green. When it stopped boiling, the man drank it down.

"A second later, he cried out with pain and began shaking and gasping for air. Then he began to change. His face grew more handsome, and his body grew larger, too. Then I jumped to my feet in terror, for there he stood—Dr. Henry Jekyll!

"I cannot tell you any more because I am too sick in body and soul. I will just say one thing, Utterson, my friend. The thing that came to my door that night was Edward Hyde."

I put down the letter from Dr. Lanyon and read the one from Dr. Jekyll:

"As a young man, my future seemed bright. My

parents were rich, and my childhood was happy. I was in good health and had a good mind. My only fault was that I really liked to have a good time. There is nothing really wrong with that, but I was ashamed of it. I wanted so much to be respected that I began to hide my little pleasures.

"As time went on, I became more and more divided. One part of me wished to do good and win respect. The other part simply wanted pleasure, even if it brought shame. Before long, I was sure that I was really two persons. One was good; the other was bad. They were always fighting inside me.

"I began to wonder if there might be a way to separate these two men. I wanted to give each one a separate body. Then each would be free to go his own way, and I would no longer be at war with myself.

"I started to test different drugs. At last, I felt I had one that would work. I knew it was dangerous, perhaps deadly, but I wanted to try it anyway. I mixed the drug with a special liquid, then drank it. I felt the most awful pain, but then I felt reborn lighter, happier, and much more reckless. I knew at once that I was far more evil than I had ever been before.

"Then I looked at myself in the mirror. I was short, ugly, and hairy, but this didn't bother me. In fact, I liked what I saw. It was the face of pure evil. I chose to call this evil person Edward Hyde.

"I then swallowed another dose of the drug, and went through the same awful pain; but when it was

over, I was myself again. I thought the drug was perfect. I could become Mr. Hyde, or change back to Dr. Jekyll, whenever I wanted.

"At first, Mr. Hyde's pleasures were the usual sort—gambling and other things. Later, Hyde became a monster, and his pleasure came from hurting other people. You know, of course, how he hurt that young girl and later murdered the old man.

"As Dr. Jekyll, I was shocked by the acts of Mr. Hyde. After the murder, I made up my mind never to become Mr. Hyde again. I stopped using the drug, and, for about two months, I was quite happy.

"Then one day, I was sitting in the park, and my body began to shake wildly. When I stopped trembling, I looked at my hands. They were crooked and covered with hair. I was shocked to realize that I had become Mr. Hyde again—without taking the drug!

"Mr. Hyde was wanted for murder. I had to change back to Dr. Jekyll. But how? I could not get back into my workroom where I kept the drug. I had locked the door used by Mr. Hyde and thrown away the key. The only other way was through the front door, but if I entered the house as Mr. Hyde, my servants would call the police.

"Then I thought of Dr. Lanyon and wrote to him, begging him to help me. You already know the rest of that story.

"My life became a nightmare. Mr. Hyde was getting stronger all the time, and Dr. Jekyll was getting

weaker. Without wanting to, I kept turning into Mr. Hyde, and I needed more and more of the drug to turn back to Dr. Jekyll. Soon I had run out of the drug!

"I shut myself up in my workroom, and I sent Poole all over the city to get more of the drug. I know now that it is useless, that the drug will no longer work. Mr. Hyde will soon take over completely.

"This is my hour of death. What will happen next will happen to Edward Hyde, not me. Will he hang for murder? Or will he have the courage to kill himself? Here then, I put down my pen and bring the unhappy life of Dr. Jekyll to an end."

ROBERT LOUIS STEVENSON

A native of Scotland, Robert Louis Stevenson (1850-1894) was ill with tuberculosis (TB) his whole life. He was often sick and had to miss school. He was able to study law, but he didn't enjoy it. So he soon quit to become a writer.

Stevenson traveled all over the world—from France to Switzerland to New York to the South Seas—looking for stories and trying to find a cure for his TB. He never did get well, and he died in Samoa at the age of 44. He did find material for many great books. The most famous are *Treasure Island*, *Kidnapped*, and *The Strange Case of Dr. Jekyll and Mr. Hyde*.

Mrs. Sappleton's husband and brothers were dead. So who was that walking across the lawn?

The Open Window

Based on the story by Saki

"My aunt will be down soon," said the 15-year-old girl. "While you wait, you must put up with me."

Framton Nuttel tried to find the right thing to say. He should be polite, of course, but he should seem to want to meet the aunt very much.

Framton was in the country to cure his nerves. His sister had wanted him to meet some people she knew there. "If you don't speak to anyone, your nerves will be worse than ever," she had told him, "and some of these people are very nice." Framton didn't think that visits to strangers would help him much. He hoped that Mrs. Sappleton, the aunt, was one of the "nice" ones.

"Do you know very many people around here?" the niece asked.

"Hardly anybody," said Framton. "My sister stayed with friends here about four years ago. She wanted me to meet some people she liked."

"Then you know almost nothing about my aunt," said the girl.

"Only her name and address," said Framton. He wondered if Mrs. Sappleton was married or a widow.

Something about the room made him think that a man lived there.

"The most terrible thing happened to her three years ago," said the girl. "It was not long after your sister was here."

"A terrible thing?" asked Framton. Terrible things seemed unlikely in this quiet country spot.

"You may be wondering why we keep that window wide open on an October afternoon," said the niece. She pointed to a large French window that opened onto a rolling green lawn.

"It's warm for this time of year," said Framton, "but does that window have anything to do with the terrible thing?"

"It all started when they went out through that window, three years ago today," the girl said mysteriously. "My aunt's husband and her two young brothers were going hunting with their little brown dog. None of them ever came back. They must have slipped into a swamp and drowned. The worst part was that their bodies were never found." Here the girl's voice started to crack. "My poor aunt! She believes that they will walk in through the window, just like they used to do. That's why she keeps the window open.

"My poor, dear aunt. She always talks about the way they went out. Her husband had his red coat over his arm. Ronnie, her younger brother, was singing an old song, 'My Bonnie Lies Over the Ocean.' He did that to tease her—it got on her nerves. You know,

sometimes, on a still, quiet evening like this, I get a creepy feeling. I almost think they will all walk in through that window. . . ."

She broke off, shaking her head. Framton was glad when the aunt came into the room, saying how sorry she was to be late.

"I hope you have enjoyed talking to Vera," she said.

"She has been very interesting," said Framton.

"I hope you don't mind the open window," said Mrs. Sappleton. "My husband and brothers will be home soon. They've been hunting, and they always come in this way. They'll have shot some birds, so they'll mess up the rug, but that's the way men are, isn't it?"

She chattered on cheerfully. She talked about hunting, and how it might be better next winter. To Framton, it was awful. He saw that Vera's aunt was not paying much attention to him. Her eyes were on the open window and the lawn. He was sorry that he had come to visit on this, of all days.

"The doctors say I should do nothing exciting and get lots of rest," Framton said, trying to change the subject. He had not yet learned that few people are interested in other people's health. "Of course, none of them agree about what I should eat."

"No?" said Mrs. Sappleton. Then her face grew brighter, but it was not because of their conversation.

"Here they are at last!" she cried. "They're just in time for tea. They look as if they were muddy right up to their eyeballs!"

Framton turned toward the niece, to give her an understanding look, but the girl was staring out through the open window. Her eyes were wide with fear.

In the gray light, three figures were walking across the lawn toward the window. They were carrying guns under their arms. One of them had a red coat over his shoulders. A tired brown dog followed close behind. They drew near the house without making a sound, but suddenly a young voice began to sing, "My Bonnie lies over the ocean . . . "

Framton jumped to his feet and ran for the door. Out in the road, a man on a bicycle had to run into a

hedge to keep from running right into him.

"Here we are, dear," said the man with the red coat, coming in through the window. "We're muddy, but most of it's dry. Who was that who ran out as we came up?"

"A very strange man, a Mr. Nuttel," said Mrs. Sappleton. "He only talked about being ill. Then he ran off without saying good-bye. You'd think he had seen a ghost."

"It was probably the dog," said Vera. "He told me he was afraid of dogs and that once he was chased into a graveyard in India by a pack of wild dogs. He had to spend the night in a grave that had just been dug, and the dogs barked and howled and snapped right above him all night. I'm sure it was enough to make anyone lose their nerve."

Making up exciting stories on short notice was Vera's specialty.

SAKI

Saki was the pen name of Hector Hugh Munro (1870-1916). He was born in Burma, but he moved to England to live with his aunts when he was only two. As an adult, he got a job as a policeman. Later, he became a newspaper reporter and traveled all around the world. He's best known for writing short stories with surprise endings like "The Open Window."

"I had no choice but to kill the old man. He had an eye like a vulture, filmy and gray."

BASED ON THE STORY BY EDGAR ALLAN POE

It's true that I am nervous, very nervous—but I'm not crazy. Listen and you'll see how calmly I can tell you the whole story.

I can't say how the idea first entered my brain, but once it was there, it haunted me day and night. There wasn't any reason for it. I liked the old man. He never did anything to hurt me, and I wasn't after his money.

I think it was his eyes! Yes, that was it! One of his eyes looked like the eye of a vulture, pale gray, with a film over it. Whenever it looked at me, my blood ran cold. Slowly, very slowly, I made up my mind to kill the old man and get rid of that eye forever.

I was never kinder to the old man than during the week before I killed him. I made my move slowly and carefully. Every night at midnight, I opened his door very gently. When I had made an opening large enough for my head, I put a lantern on the floor. The lantern was turned off so that no light showed. Then I pushed my head into the room. It took me an hour to place my whole head in so that I could see him lying on his bed. Ha! Would a madman have been so smart? Then,

when my head was all the way into the room, I picked up the lantern and turned it on carefully, so just one ray of light could fall on his vulture eye.

I did this for seven nights—every night just at midnight. But his eye was always closed, so I could not do what I had to do. It was not the old man who bothered me. It was his evil eye.

Every morning I calmly went into his room and asked him if he had slept well. So you see, he would never suspect that every night, just at midnight, I looked in on him as he slept.

On the eighth night, I was even more careful than usual. Never before had I realized how smart I was, or felt the power that I had. When I thought about the fact that I was opening the door and that he was not even dreaming of my secret thoughts, I had to laugh to myself.

Perhaps he heard me. He moved suddenly. Now you may think I moved, too, but I didn't. His room was dark, so I knew he could not see the door opening.

I had my head in and was about to turn the lantern on, but my thumb slipped on the tin switch. The old man sat up in bed, crying, "Who's there?"

I kept still, not moving an inch. Finally I heard a slight groan, and I knew it was a groan of terror—terror in the face of death. It was not a groan of pain or grief but the low, choking sound that comes from the bottom of the soul. I knew the sound well, as many a night, when all the world slept, it had come from me.

I knew the terror that the old man felt and I pitied him, although I laughed inside. I knew he had been lying awake ever since the first slight noise. His fears had grown ever since. He tried to tell himself, "It is nothing but the wind in the chimney. . . . It is only a mouse crossing the floor. . . . It is just a cricket."

Yes, he was trying to comfort himself, but death was approaching with its black shadow. That shadow made the old man feel my presence in the room.

I waited a long time, and then I turned the lantern up a little bit. I was careful. Only a single ray shot out and fell on his vulture eye.

The eye was wide open! I grew angry as I looked at it. I could see it perfectly—that dull gray with an ugly film over it chilled my bones.

Then I heard it, a low, dull, quick sound. It was like the sound a watch makes when it's wrapped in cotton; it was the beating of the old man's heart. It made my anger grow, but even then I kept still. I hardly breathed at all. I kept the ray of light shining on his eye. The beating of his heart grew quicker and quicker, and louder and louder.

I told you that I am nervous, and it's true. In the dead hour of the night, in the awful silence of that old house, that noise terrified me. Yet for a few minutes longer, I stood still.

The beating grew louder, louder! Then a new fear grabbed me. The sound was so loud that a neighbor might hear it!

The old man's hour had come! With a loud yell, I turned the lantern up and leaped into the room. He screamed once, only once, before I dragged him to the floor and pulled the heavy bed over him.

I smiled. The deed was almost done. For many minutes his heart beat on with a muffled sound. This didn't bother me. The sound would not be heard through the wall.

Finally it stopped, and the old man was dead. I removed the bed and looked at the body. I put my hand on his heart and held it there many minutes—no heartbeat. His eye would not trouble me ever again.

If you still think I'm crazy, you won't think so after I tell you the smart way that I hid the body. I worked quickly but silently as I pulled up three boards from the floor. Then I slipped the body into the space below and replaced the boards so well that no human eye could have found anything wrong. Ha ha!

Soon after I'd finished, someone knocked at the door. I went to open it with a light heart. I had nothing to fear.

Three policemen came in and said that a neighbor had heard a scream and had gone to the police station.

I smiled and invited them in. The scream, I said, was my own. I'd had a nightmare. I told them that the old man was away in the country, and I took them all over the house. I told them to search it—search it well.

Finally, I took them into his room and asked them to sit down. I placed my own chair on the floorboards above his body.

The policemen were satisfied since I seemed very much at ease. We talked about all sorts of things.

Before long, though, I felt myself getting pale, and I wanted them to leave. My head hurt and I imagined a pounding in my ears, but the policemen just sat there, talking and talking. The pounding in my ears grew louder. I talked faster to get rid of it, but it kept getting louder. Finally, I decided that the terrible noise was not just in my head.

I grew pale and tried talking more quickly and in a louder voice, but the sound got louder, too. What

could I do? It was a low, dull, quick sound. It was like the sound a watch makes when it is wrapped in cotton.

I gasped for breath. The police didn't seem to hear the sound, so I kept talking, even more quickly now. The noise got louder, but what could I do? I raved and swore and scraped my chair over the floorboards. Still the noise grew louder and louder!

The men kept talking and smiling. Was it possible that they did not hear? No, they heard, and they knew! They were making fun of my terror.

Anything was better than this. I couldn't stand their smiles any longer. I had to scream—or I'd die. The noise was louder, louder, louder!

"Enough!" I screamed. "I admit it! Tear up the floor! Here, here! It is the beating of his hideous heart!"

Edgar Allan Poe

Edgar Allan Poe (1809-1849), one of the first people to write horror stories and mysteries, was born in Boston. His father deserted the family, and his mother died when he was only three. A Baltimore family raised him but never adopted him.

By the time Poe was 18 years old, he was living in the streets. His early life and later mental illness influenced the sorts of things he wrote—strange horror tales such as "The Tell-Tale Heart." Although people today recognize Poe as a genius, he lived in poverty all his life and died alone in the streets.

Mr. White had a very simple dream. It was about to turn into a nightmare.

The Monkey's Paw

Based on the story by W. W. Jacobs

Outside, the night was cold and wet, but in the Whites' living room, a fire burned brightly. Father and son were playing chess. "Listen to the wind," said Mr. White. He'd made a bad move, and he was hoping his son Herbert wouldn't notice.

"I hear it," said Herbert, taking advantage of his father's mistake. "Check."

"I don't think that my old friend will make it here tonight," said Mr. White, making another move.

"Checkmate," replied his son, as he won the game.

"That's the worst part of living so far out," said Mr. White. "The road is always washed out."

"Never mind, dear," said his wife. "Perhaps you'll win the next game."

Just then, the gate banged loudly, and heavy footsteps came toward the door.

"Your friend made it after all," said Herbert.

The old man got up and opened the door. Then he led his friend into the living room.

"This is Major Morris," he said. "He was in the army. He's been everywhere and seen everything."

Morris shook hands and sat down by the fire. As he warmed up, his eyes got brighter. He began to talk. Everyone listened as he told stories about strange scenes, bloody wars, and horrible plagues.

"He's been gone 21 years," said Mr. White, nodding at his wife and son. "When he went away, he was a young man working with me in the warehouse. I'd like to travel, too, you know."

"You're better off where you are," said Morris, shaking his head. He put down his empty glass.

"I'd like to see old temples and mysterious objects," said the old man. "What were you telling me the other day? Something about a monkey's paw?"

"Oh, that was nothing," said Morris quickly.

"Monkey's paw?" asked Mrs. White.

"It's nothing. It's just something that they think is magic over in a faraway country," said Morris.

The White family leaned forward. Morris absentmindedly put his empty glass to his lips and then set it down again. Mr. White filled it for him.

"I think I've got the stupid thing here," said Morris, pulling something out of his pocket. "It looks just like an ordinary paw, all dried up."

Mrs. White drew back, but her son took it and looked at it curiously.

"What's special about it?" asked Mr. White. He took it from his son and set it down on the table.

"An old man put a spell on it," said Morris. "He wanted to show that fate ruled people's lives, and that

those who interfered would regret it. The spell grants three separate people three wishes."

"So are you going to try it?" asked Herbert.

"I have," Morris said quietly, and his face whitened.

"Did your wishes come true?" asked Mrs. White.

"They did," said Morris, and his glass tapped against his teeth.

"Has anybody else tried it?" asked Mrs. White.

"The first man had his three wishes. I don't know what the first two were, but the third was for death. That's how I got the paw."

His voice sounded so sad that the others grew quiet.

"If you've had your three wishes, then it's no good to you now," said Mr. White at last. "Why do you still have it?"

Morris shook his head. "I thought once that I would sell it, but I probably won't. It has caused enough trouble, and besides, people won't buy it. Some think it's a fairy tale. Others want to try it first and pay me later."

"If you could have another three wishes," asked Mr. White, "would you want them?"

Morris didn't answer. He just took the paw and threw it into the fire. Mr. White, with a little cry, bent and snatched it out of the flames.

"Better let it burn," said Morris.

"If you don't want it," said Mr. White, "why not give it to me?"

"No. I threw it on the fire. If you keep it, don't blame me for what happens. Throw it back, please."

The old man shook his head and stared at the paw. "How do you do it?"

"Hold it up in your right hand and wish aloud," said Morris, "but I'm telling you not to do it."

"It does sound like a fairy tale," said Mrs. White, as she got up and began to put the dinner on the table. "Why don't you wish for four pairs of hands for me?"

Mr. White held up the monkey's paw as Morris, looking alarmed, caught him by the arm. "If you must wish," he said, "wish for something sensible."

Mr. White dropped the paw into his pocket and led his friend to the table. As everyone ate, they all forgot about the paw. Then, after dinner, they sat listening as Morris told more stories about his adventures.

Finally, they closed the door behind their guest. "If the story about the monkey's paw isn't any more truthful than his other tall tales," said Mr. White, "there's not much to it."

"Did you give him anything for it?" asked his wife.

"Not much. He didn't want it, but I made him take it. He begged me again to throw the thing away."

"Wish to be a king, Father," said Herbert. "Then nobody can boss you around."

Mr. White took the paw from his pocket and eyed it doubtfully. "I don't know what to wish for," he said. "I've really got all I want."

"If you paid off the mortgage on the house, you'd be completely happy," said Herbert. "Wish for 2,000 dollars to do that."

Mr. White held up the paw. His son sat down at the piano, and laughing, struck a few impressive chords.

"I wish for 2,000 dollars" said the old man. Then he let out a strange little cry and dropped the paw to the floor.

His wife and son ran toward him.

"It moved," he said. "As I wished, it twisted in my hands like a snake."

"Well, I don't see the 2,000 dollars," said his son, picking up the paw and putting it on the table. "And I bet I never do."

"That's impossible. You must have just imagined

it," said his wife, looking at him anxiously.

He shook his head. "No, I felt it move. I'm all right, but it gave me a shock just the same." Then he felt cold . . . and a little afraid.

The next morning, the sun streamed over the breakfast table, and Mr. White laughed at his fears. The room looked cheery, and the shriveled old paw lay on the counter, looking completely ordinary.

"I suppose all old soldiers are the same," said Mrs. White. "How could we have listened to that nonsense? How could three wishes be granted? If they could, how could getting the mortgage money hurt you?"

"The money might drop on his head from the sky," said Herbert.

"Morris said that everything happens so naturally," said his father, "that you might think it was all just a big coincidence."

"Well, don't spend all the money before I come back," said Herbert, rising from the table. "I'm afraid it'll turn you into a greedy old man."

"Herbert will make more funny remarks when he comes home from work," Mrs. White said after her son had been gone awhile.

"I wouldn't be surprised," said Mr. White, "but the thing really did move in my hand. I'd swear to that."

"At least, you *thought* it moved."

"It did," he said. Then he looked up at his wife, who

was staring out the window. "What's the matter?"

She didn't answer. She was watching a man, who seemed to be trying to decide whether or not to knock on their door. She noticed that he was well dressed and wearing an expensive suit. Three times he walked past their gate, then turned and walked back. The fourth time, he opened the gate and walked up the path. Mrs. White got up and opened the door.

She brought the man into the house and waited for him to say something. At first, he was silent. "I was asked to come here," he said at last, stooping to pick lint off his pants. "I'm from Maw and Meggins."

Mrs. White was startled. "Is anything the matter?" she asked anxiously. "Has anything happened to Herbert at work?"

Her husband interrupted. "There, there," he said. "Don't jump to conclusions. You're not bringing us bad news, are you?" he asked the man.

"I'm sorry . . ."

"Is he hurt?" demanded Mrs. White.

The man nodded. "Badly hurt," he said quietly, "but he is not in any pain."

"Oh, thank heavens!" said the old woman. "Thank heavens for that! Thank—"

She broke off suddenly as she realized what the man really meant. Herbert was dead. She caught her breath, and turning to her husband, put her trembling hand on his. There was a long silence.

"I'm afraid that he was caught in the machinery

this morning," said the man finally.

"Caught in the machinery," repeated Mr. White.

He sat, staring blankly out the window, and pressed his wife's hand between his own.

"He was the only son we had," he said, turning to the visitor. "It is hard."

The man coughed and walked slowly to the window. "The firm wanted me to give you their sincere sympathy," he said, not looking around. "Please understand that I am only an employee, and I'm only obeying orders."

Neither Mr. or Mrs. White replied. Their faces were white, their eyes staring.

"They told me to say that Maw and Meggins is not responsible for what happened. Still, they want to present you with a certain sum of money."

Mr. White gazed with horror at the visitor. His dry lips shaped the words, "How much?"

"Two thousand dollars."

Mr. White didn't even hear his wife's scream. He smiled faintly, put out his hands like a blind man, and fell to the floor.

The Whites buried their son in a huge new cemetery two miles away. They came back to a house filled with shadows and silence. It was all over so quickly that at first they could hardly believe it. They kept waiting for something else to happen, something to make their lives easier to bear.

About a week after the funeral, Mr. White woke up

in the middle of the night. He stretched out his hand and found himself alone in the darkness. He heard his wife weeping by the window. "Come back," he said tenderly. "You will be cold."

"It is colder for my son," she said and kept crying.

He went back to sleep until a sudden wild cry from his wife woke him with a start. "The monkey's paw!" she cried wildly. "The monkey's paw!"

He looked up in alarm. "Where is it? What's happened. What's the matter?"

She stumbled across the room toward him. "I want it," she said. "You haven't destroyed it, have you?"

"It's in the living room. Why?"

She bent over and kissed his cheek. "Why didn't I think of it before? Why didn't you think of it?"

"Think of what?"

"The other two wishes. We've only had one."

"Wasn't that enough?"

"No," she said. "We'll have one more. Go down and get the monkey's paw, and wish our son alive again."

The man sat up in bed and threw off the covers. "You're crazy!"

"We had the first wish granted," said Mrs. White. "Why not the second?"

"A coincidence," he stammered.

"Go and get it!"

Mr. White's voice shook. "I don't think you want him back. He has been dead 10 days. When he was killed, he was so mangled that I could only recognize

him by his clothing."

"Bring him back," she demanded. "Do you think I'm afraid of my own child?"

He went down in the darkness, and felt his way to the living room. He found the monkey's paw on the mantel. Then he felt his way along the wall until he found himself in the hall.

Even his wife's face seemed different as he entered the room. He was almost afraid of her. "Wish!" she cried, in a strong voice.

"It is foolish and wrong," he protested.

"Wish!" she repeated.

He raised his hand. "I wish my son alive again."

The monkey's paw jerked in his hand and fell to the floor. He sank into a chair as his wife walked to the window and opened the blinds.

He sat until he was chilled with the cold. He glanced now and then at his wife peering through the window. The candle threw shadows on the ceiling and walls until, finally, it flickered out. Nothing happened. Their son did not come back. Mr. White crawled back to bed with a sense of relief. A minute or two later, his wife lay down silently beside him.

Neither spoke, but both lay listening to the ticking of the clock. A stair creaked, and a squeaky mouse scurried through the wall. The darkness bothered the old man. Finally, he took the box of matches and, striking one, went downstairs for a candle.

At the foot of the stairs, the match went out. He

stopped to strike another. At that moment, he heard a knock on the front door.

The matches fell from his hand. He stood motionless, not breathing until he heard the knock again. Then he turned, ran back to his room, and closed the door behind him. A third knock sounded through the house.

"What's that?" cried Mrs. White.

"A rat," said Mr. White, shaking. "A rat passed me on the stairs."

His wife sat up in bed, listening. The knocking started again.

"It's Herbert!" she screamed. "It's Herbert!"

She ran to the door, but her husband got there before her. He caught her by the arm in the hallway and held her tightly.

"What are you going to do?" he whispered.

"It's my boy. It's Herbert!" she cried. "I forgot the cemetery was two miles away. That's what took so long! Why are you holding me back? Let go. I have to open the door."

"Don't let it in," cried Mr. White, trembling.

"You're afraid of your own son. Let me go. I'm coming, Herbert!"

There was another knock and another. Mrs. White pulled free and ran from the room. Her husband had reached the landing when he heard her voice, strained and panting.

"The door bolt! Come help me. It's too high for me to reach."

But her husband was on his hands and knees. He was reaching wildly for the paw. If he could only find it before the thing outside got in. He heard a chair scrape as his wife put it down in front of the door. He heard the creaking of the door bolt as she pushed it back. At the same moment, he found the monkey's paw. He frantically made his third and last wish.

The knocking stopped suddenly, although its echoes were still in the house. He heard the door open, and a cold wind rushed up the stairs. His wife's long, loud wail of misery gave him the courage to run to her side. He looked out the door and past the gate. The street lamp shone on a quiet and deserted road.

W. W. JACOBS

William Wymark Jacobs (1863-1943) was born in London, England. He began writing stories while he was a young man working in the post office. Most of them were about the sea and sailors. He gathered his material by hanging around the wharf where his father worked. Despite his interest in the sailing life, it was this classic horror story, "The Monkey's Paw," that made him famous.

He was surrounded by the world's worst killers. Fortunately, they were only statues—or were they?

BASED ON THE STORY BY A.M. BURRAGE

The guards at the Museum of Waxworks were sending the last visitors out. In his office, the manager sat talking to Raymond Hewson.

The manager was a young man. He wore his clothes well and tried to look stylish. Raymond Hewson looked the opposite. His clothes had been good when new, but they showed signs of wear. He was a small, pale man with brown hair, and he had a defensive air. He had talent, but he was a failure because he had absolutely no self-confidence.

"There is nothing new about your request," the manager said. "In fact, we turn people down about three times a week. We have nothing to gain by letting people spend the night in our 'Murderers' Den.' If I allowed it, and some young idiot lost his mind, I'd lose my job. But the fact that you're a reporter makes it a little different."

Hewson smiled. "I suppose you mean that reporters have no minds to lose."

"No, no," laughed the manager, "but they're responsible people. Besides, here we do have

something to gain: publicity."

"Exactly," said Hewson.

"What paper do you work for, Mr. Hewson?"

"I'm working for myself at present," Hewson confessed, "writing articles for several papers. I'll have no trouble getting the story printed. The *Morning Echo* would use it in an instant. 'A Night with Murderers'—no paper could turn it down."

The manager rubbed his chin. "What would the article be like?"

"I'd make it gruesome, of course—gruesome with a little bit of humor."

The manager nodded. "Very well, Mr. Hewson. Get your story printed in the *Morning Echo*, and we'll pay you 200 dollars. Still, I wouldn't want to do what you're doing. Those wax figures don't bother me while the museum is open, but I'd hate to have to sleep down there alone with them."

"Why?" asked Hewson.

"I don't know. I don't believe in ghosts, but I just couldn't sit with those figures all night, with their eyes staring the way they do. After all, they were the worst people in the world. The whole atmosphere of the place is unpleasant. If atmosphere affects you, you'll have a *very* unpleasant night."

Hewson had known *that* from the moment the idea first occurred to him. He felt sick, even while he smiled at the manager. Still, he had a family to support. Here was a chance to earn the money for a story in the

Morning Echo, plus 200 dollars from the museum. That would keep him going for two weeks. Besides, if he wrote the story well, it might even lead to a full-time job.

"I expect to have an uncomfortable night," said Hewson. "'The Murderers' Den' is not a hotel room, but I don't think your waxworks will worry me."

"You're not superstitious?"

"Not a bit." Hewson laughed.

"Yet you're a writer. You must have an extremely vivid imagination," the manager said.

"The editors I write for have always complained that I don't. You see, readers of newspapers want more than just the facts," Hewson said.

The manager smiled. "Right," he said. "I think the last customers have gone. I'll let the night watchmen know that you'll be here. Then I'll take you down and show you around."

He made a quick phone call. Then he said, "Now, if you're ready, we'll go downstairs."

Hewson followed the manager through half a dozen rooms, past the wax figures of kings and queens, generals and politicians. The manager stopped once and spoke to a man in uniform, saying something about a chair in the Murderers' Den.

"It's the best we can do for you, I'm afraid," he said to Hewson. "I hope you'll be able to get some sleep."

He led the way downstairs, through a dark hallway, and into the Murderers' Den.

It was an oddly shaped room with a high ceiling and dim light. The waxwork murderers stood on low pedestals. Recent murderers stood next to "old favorites." The manager pointed out a few of the murderers to Hewson.

"Who's that one over there?" Hewson interrupted in a whisper, pointing.

"That is our star," said the manager. "He's the only one of the bunch who hasn't been hanged."

The figure was a small man wearing a cape. The face looked so evil that Hewson had to force himself to look at it.

"Who is he?" he asked again.

"That," said the manager, "is Dr. Bourdette."

"I think I've heard the name," Hewson said, "but I can't remember what he did."

"You'd remember if you were a Frenchman," the manager said. "For some time, he was the terror of Paris. He was a doctor who healed people by day and cut throats by night. After his last crime, he left a clue behind that put the police on his trail. One clue led to another, and before long, they had enough evidence to have him hanged—or sent to a mental hospital.

"Even then, he was too clever for them. When he realized that they were closing in on him, he disappeared. Ever since, police all over the world have been looking for him. Many people think that he killed himself, but his body has never been found. One or two crimes like his have been committed since then,

but experts think they were done by an imitator."

Hewson shuddered. "I don't like him at all," he confessed. "What eyes he has!"

"Yes, this figure is a masterpiece. Do you find the eyes biting into you? Bourdette used his eyes to hypnotize his victims before cutting their throats. There were never any signs of a struggle."

"I thought I saw him move," said Hewson, with a catch in his voice.

The manager smiled. "Your eyes will play a number of tricks on you before the night is over, I expect. You won't be locked in. You can go upstairs when you've had enough. The watchmen are here, so you'll have company. Don't be alarmed if you hear them walking around. One of the watchmen will bring a chair down here for you. I wish you well, Mr. Hewson."

The night watchman who brought a chair for Hewson was amused. "Where shall I put it?" he asked, grinning. "Which murderer would you like to keep you company this evening?"

Hewson smiled. The man's joking pleased him because it made everything seem normal. "I'll put it somewhere myself, thanks," he said.

"Well, good night. I'll be upstairs. Don't let them sneak up behind you and touch your neck with their cold, clammy hands."

Hewson laughed and told the man good night. He turned the armchair around so its back was toward

the figure of Dr. Bourdette. For some reason he did not like this particular figure.

The rows of figures in the dim light looked so human that the silence seemed unreal. He missed the sound of breathing and the rustling of clothes.

He faced the figures boldly. They were only waxworks, but he was sure that Dr. Bourdette was staring at the back of his head. The eyes of the little doctor haunted him, and he felt he must turn and look.

"No," he thought. "If I turn and look, I'll be admitting how scared I am."

Then another voice in his brain spoke to him.

"You're not turning around because you're afraid."

The two voices argued for a moment or two. Then Hewson turned and looked behind him.

The figure of the dreadful little doctor stood out from all the others. Perhaps this was because a beam of light fell right on it. Hewson looked into the eyes for one painful second and then turned away again.

"He's only a waxwork like the rest of you," Hewson muttered to himself.

They were only waxworks, yes, but waxworks don't move. He hadn't actually seen them move, but he felt their positions had changed while his back was turned. Hewson remembered the words of his editors, and he laughed bitterly. "And they tell me that I've got no imagination!" he said under his breath.

He took a notebook from his pocket and wrote: "Dr. Bourdette's eyes are hypnotic. The figures seem to move when not being watched."

He closed the notebook and looked quickly over his right shoulder. He hadn't seen anything move, but he was sure something had. He stared straight into the face of one of the figures. It looked back as if to say, "I wasn't the one who moved."

Of course, none of them had moved. It was just his own nerves. Or was it?

Hewson started to get up from the chair. He wasn't going to spend the night with a lot of waxworks that moved around when he wasn't looking.

Hewson sat down again. This was silly. They were

only waxworks. Then why was he so sure that something was happening—just out of his sight?

He swung around quickly to meet the stare of Dr. Bourdette. The figure wasn't moving.

He told himself he ought to leave. Already he had experienced enough to write his story, or ten stories.

Yes, but that watchman upstairs would laugh at him. The manager might not give him the 200 dollars that he needed so badly. His wife would laugh, too, when he told her what he had imagined.

Wait! Somebody was breathing. Or was it the sound of his own breath? He sat still and held his breath. Finally he let it out with a sigh. It was his own breathing he had heard, after all. Or was somebody breathing only when he breathed?

He must stop this! He must get his mind on something normal. He was Raymond Hewson, a newspaper writer. These figures around him were made of wax and sawdust. That was better! Now, what was that funny story he had heard at lunch yesterday?

He remembered part of it, but not all of it, because he turned around to look at Dr. Bourdette again.

Now Hewson was staring into those dreadful, hypnotic eyes. His own eyes were open wide, and his mouth was twisted in a snarl.

"You moved!" he cried. "Yes, you did! I saw you!"

Then he sat quite still, staring straight ahead, like a man found frozen in the snow. Those eyes had hypnotized him.

Dr. Bourdette moved slowly. He stepped off his pedestal. Then nodded and said, "Good evening."

He continued to speak in perfect English. "I did not know that I would have the pleasure of your company tonight." Even his voice was hypnotic. "You cannot move or speak unless I tell you to, but you can hear me. Please do not be nervous. I am not a waxwork that has come to life. I am Dr. Bourdette himself. The manager's description of me was not entirely right. I am not dead, although the world thinks I am."

He paused and stretched his legs. Then he went on.

"Pardon me. I am a little stiff. Let me explain. I was close to this building this afternoon when I saw a policeman staring at me. I thought he might ask me some questions, so I mingled with the crowd and came in here. Then I had a wonderful idea.

"I yelled 'Fire!' When all the fools had rushed upstairs, I took the cape off the waxwork of myself. I put it around my shoulders and hid the waxwork in the back. Then I took its place on the pedestal.

"I have spent a very tiring evening here. I could breathe only when I wasn't being watched. One small boy screamed and said he saw me moving. I heard his parents say he would be punished when he got home."

He paused and looked at Hewson's throat. Then he went on.

"I am thankful for the good luck that brought us together tonight, and I should not complain."

From an inside pocket, he took out a small razor.

DID YOU LIKE THIS BOOK?

Here are two other READ 180 Paperbacks that you might like to read.

WAIT UNTIL DARK

Lock your doors. Check your closet. Look under your bed. Now, you might be ready to read this collection of scary stories.

BY J.B. STAMPER

DESTINATION: EVEREST

Climbing Mount Everest, the highest mountain in the world, had always been Josh's dream. But will he manage to get off the mountain alive?

BY KAREN GLENN

"This razor has a very narrow blade," he remarked. "It does not cut very deeply, but deeply enough. In just one moment, you will see for yourself."

He stood up and walked over to Hewson.

"Please raise your chin a little. Thank you. Just a little more. Ah, thank you!"

After sunrise, a few weak rays of sunshine shone through a window. The waxwork figures still stood in their places. In the middle of them, Hewson sat motionless. His chin was tilted up, as if he were waiting for a barber to shave him. There was not a scratch on his throat or anywhere else on his body. Yet he was cold and dead. The editors he used to work for were wrong when they said that he had no imagination.

Dr. Bourdette was standing on his pedestal. He did not move, nor was he able to move. After all, he was only a waxwork.

A.M. BURRAGE

Not much is known about Alfred McLellan Burrage, a man who was as mysterious as his stories. His first collection of ghostly tales was published in 1927. Burrage wrote often about an "occult detective" named Francis Chard who, like the characters in *The X-Files*, investigated weird phenomena. Just to make himself even more mysterious, Burrage also had a pseudonym—ex-Private X.